Park Beat

Rhymin' Through the Seasons

By Jonathan London

Illustrated by Woodleigh Marx Hubbard

HarperCollins Publishers

Park Beat
Text copyright © 2001 by Jonathan London
Illustrations copyright © 2001 by Woodleigh Marx Hubbard
Printed in the U.S.A. All rights reserved.
www.harperchildrens.com

Library of Congress Cataloging-in-Publication Data
London, Jonathan.
    Park beat / by Jonathan London ; illustrated by Woodleigh Marx Hubbard.
        p.   cm.
    Summary: Rhyming text describes activities and sights during the four seasons.
    ISBN 0-688-13994-9 (trade). — ISBN 0-688-13995-7 (lib. bdg.)
    [1. Seasons—Fiction.   2. Stories in rhyme.]   I. Hubbard, Woodleigh, ill.   II. Title.
PZ8.3.L8433Wal   2000   99-27643
[E]—dc21   CIP
                                                                                                                    AC

Typography by Robbin Gourley
3   4   5   6   7   8   9   10
❖

For all our all-seasons walkin'-and-talkin' friends, Bob & Pat & Leah,
Michelle & Christine, & Gerard, with thanks to Sean —J.L.

In joyful and loving memory of Coriander 8 and Blake 6 —W.M.H.

The illustrator would like to express gratitude to Melanie Donovan,
Golda Laurens, and Andrea Brown; with special huzzahs for my wildly
supportive friends, Katrina and Isa.

**Dogs yappin' and geese flappin',
Fish jumpin' and apples thumpin',**

Squirrels blatherin' and nut-gatherin',

Gardeners reapin' and cornstalks heapin',
Branches rattlin' and fires cracklin',

**Pumpkins grinnin' and spiders spinnin',
Wind howlin' and goblins prowlin',**

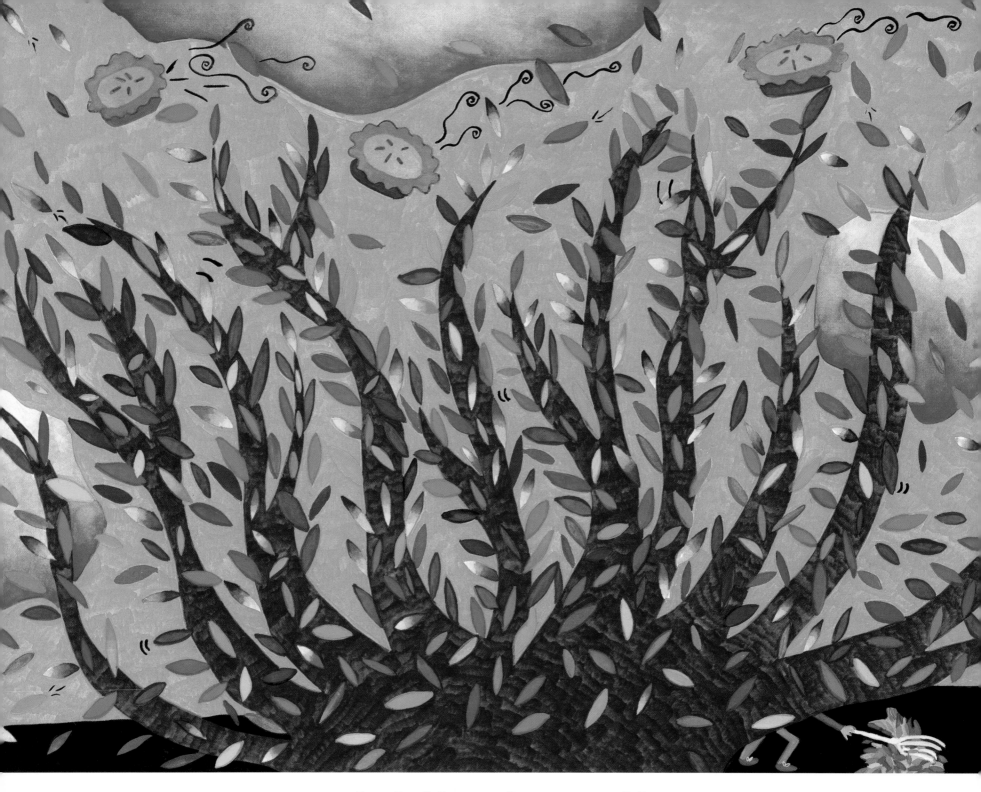

Pies bakin' and Papa's rakin',

Leaves fallin' and Mama's callin',

I'm runnin' and flyin'—*wheeee! crash!*
And now I'm lyin' in a pile of leaves,

Rappin' and tappin' and finger-snappin'
On a walk through fall.

Breath steamin' and icicles gleamin',
Scarves blowin' and candles glowin',

Mittens missin' and skaters kissin',

Sleigh bells jinglin' and fingers tinglin',
Sleds slidin' and some collidin',

Kids shakin' and angel-makin',

Papa's plowin' and dog's bowwowin',

Snow's fallin' and Mama's callin',

**Snowballs flyin'—*zing! oof!*
And now I'm lyin' in a pile of snow,**

Rappin' and tappin' and finger-snappin'
On a walk through winter.

**Birds chirpin' and frogs burpin',
Creek's flowin' and flowers growin',**

**Crickets bouncin' and kittens pouncin',
Gardeners putterin' and butterflies flutterin',**

Clouds bloomin' and storm's loomin',

Rain's fallin' and Mama's callin',

I'm slippin' and slidin'—*oops! yikes!*
And now I'm glidin' in a puddle of mud,

**Rappin' and tappin' and finger-snappin'
On a walk through spring.**

**Ducks cruisin' and turtles snoozin',
Flickers drummin' and honeybees hummin',**

Kids berry-pickin' and ice-cream-lickin',

**Ballplayers sweatin' and hot sun's settin',
Sprinklers sprinklin' and wind chimes tinklin',**

Hot dogs roastin' and skaters coastin',

Papa's loungin' and dog's scroungin',

Night's fallin' and Mama's callin',

Fireflies flashin'—*wheeee! smack!* And now I'm splashin' in our backyard pool, Rappin' and tappin' and finger-snappin' on a walk through summer.